D1281051

THE RUNAWAY SARDINE

TOLD AND ILLUSTRATED BY
EMMA L. BROCK

ALFRED A. KNOPF : NEW YORK

THIS IS A BORZOI BOOK,
PUBLISHED BY ALFRED A. KNOPF, INC.

TWELFTH PRINTING SEPTEMBER, 1951

MANUFACTURED IN THE UNITED STATES OF AMERICA

To
BOB
and
SHEILA

THE RUNAWAY SARDINE

There lived an old fisherman and his old wife in a town at the edge of the sea and that town was in Brittany.

And in the kitchen they had a yellow cat and a black hen and a sardine in a tub.

One morning after breakfast the old fisherman clumped down to the port to watch the boats on the sea and the old wife

put on her second-best apron and went to market to buy carrots and toma-toes.

The cat wa
asleep by th
fireplace
and the
black hen
was roost
ing on the to
of the bed
That left
the sardin
all alone
swimming back and forth in his tub
bumping his nose on the sides. Eac
time he bumped he wished himself

back in the
big ocean
again.
"Oh, dear,"
Zacharie
said – that
was his name
– "Oh, dear,
oh, dear!"
And then
Zacharie jumped
right out of the tub.
He took his tail in his mouth and
rolled through the door into the

street and over the cobble stones, faster and faster until he was out of breath. He stopped in front of a doorway and spied a bowl of water o[n] the sill. Zacharie thought a breath of water would feel good, so he flopped himself into it. Just then he saw [a] white cat's face peeping over the edg[e] at him.

The cat was smiling and licking his whiskers and purring out loud, "A fine sardine for my dinner!"

But Zacharie was too quick for him and jumped out of the bowl, crying "Don't catch me. I'm looking for the sea." He took his tail in his mouth and rolled into the street and over the

cobbles
and left
the
white
cat
behind.

He rolled along the Stree
BUTTER
SQUARE
E.L.BROCK

of the Red Cap and into Butter Square and between the feet of Yann the bagpipe blower and tipped him over.

"My, what a fine fish for my dinner," cried Yann as his wooden shoes flew every which way.

E.L.BROCK

But Zacharie rolled away from him and ran straight into the door of a house. There was a baby asleep in a cradle. The mother in a tall white cap was working at her spinning and singing to her baby.

When she saw Zacharie she threw her distaff at him and cried, "What a fine sardine for my dinner!"

But Zacharie was too quick for her and dodged out of the way, crying, "Don't catch me. I'm looking for the sea." He took his tail in his mouth and rolled out of the door and over the cobbles and left the woman behind.

He rolled faster and faster along this street and along that street until he was in a buckwheat field. The farmers were threshing and sifting the buckwheat.

Zacharie looked all around for the sea and found that he had missed it. It was on the other side of the town.

So just as the farmers spied him and began to shout, "Catch that sardine for our dinner!" Zacharie took his tail in his mouth and rolled out of the field and....

E.L.BROCK

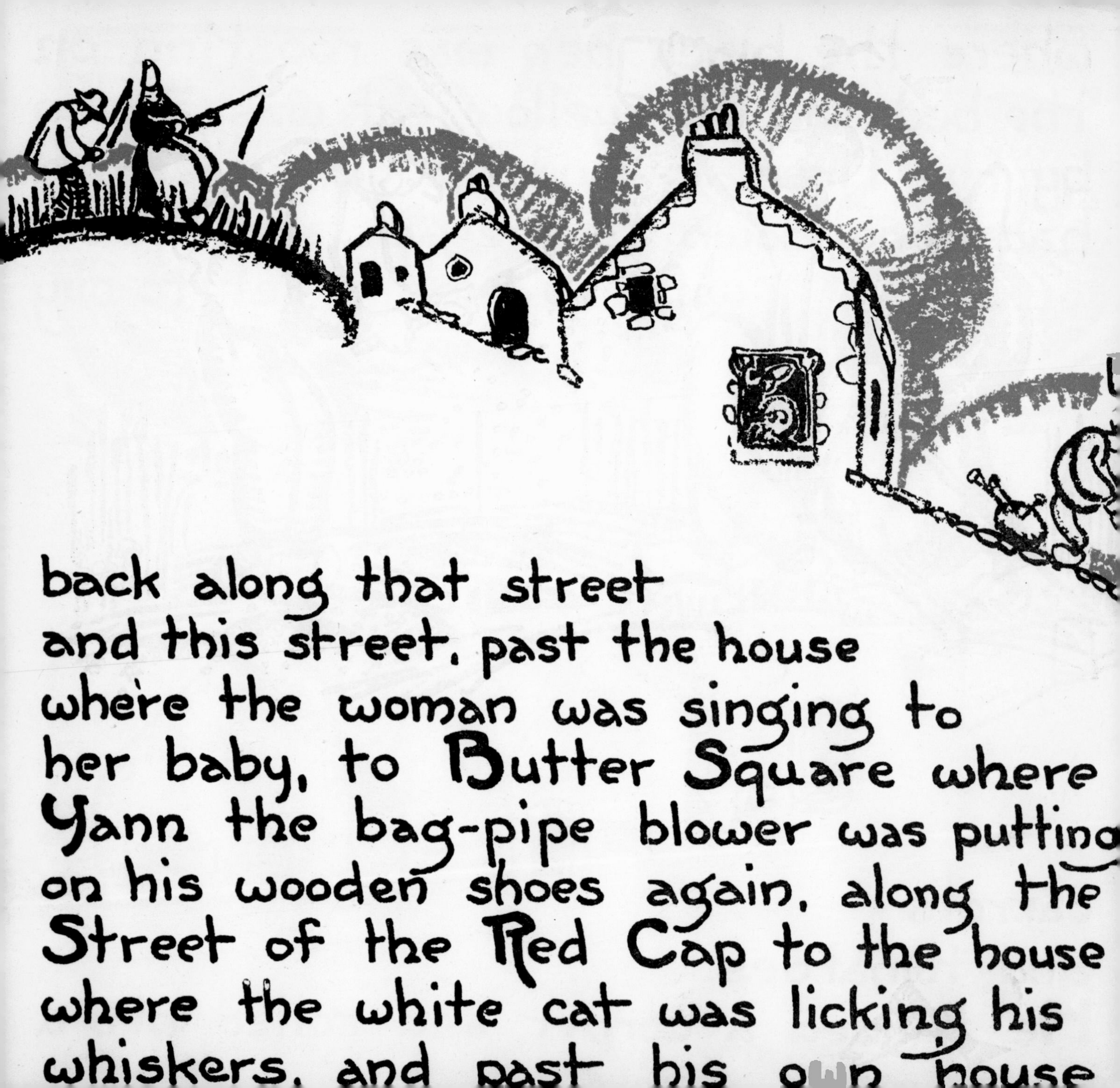

back along that street
and this street, past the house
where the woman was singing to
her baby, to Butter Square where
Yann the bag-pipe blower was putting
on his wooden shoes again, along the
Street of the Red Cap to the house
where the white cat was licking his
whiskers, and past his own house

where the black hen was roosting on the bed and the yellow cat was asleep by the fireplace and the old fisherman had gone down to the sea and the old wife to the market to buy

carrots

and tomatoes.

He turned a corner and rolled into a

little house where the goodwife was cooking crêpes. The house was dark and cool and had

an earthen floor and a row of cupboard beds all around the room except where the fireplace was. A big black kettle of soup was stewing over the fire and the goodwife was baking crêpes on a griddle. They were as thin as lace and as crisp as sugar and bigger than the moon.

Zacharie rested in a corner, but the goodwife spied him and threw her spreader at him. "A fine sardine for my dinner," cried she and started after him, spilling the crêpes all over the room. But Zacharie was too quick for her.

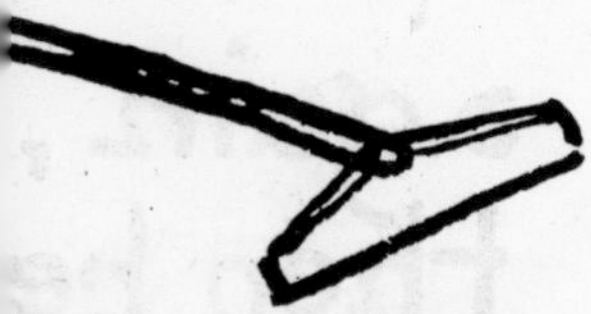

"Oh, you can't catch me. I'm looking for the sea." He tucked his tail in his mouth and rolled out of the door and left the goodwife behind.

He rolled along until he came to a street with a gutter running full of wate in the middle of it. He jumped in to catch his breath again, but just then he saw Gyp the pup-
-py

olling his tongue out at him. "Don't catch me. I'm looking for the sea," cried Zacharie and swam down the gutter and rolled up the next street and around this corner and that and up the hill to the Pig Market. The pigs were all squealing in different voices and the peasants were pushing and pulling them and trying to take them home.

Then one peasant saw Zacharie and cried, "Oh, what a fine fish for our dinner." But Zacharie was too quick for them and jumped out of reach crying, "Don't catch me, I'm looking for the sea!" He took his tail in his mouth and rolled out of the Pig Market and left the peasants behind.

RKS
EMMA L. BROCK

Zacharie stood on his tail and looked all around him for the sea, but he had missed it. It was at the other end of the town.

He started rolling back down the hill around this corner and that and along the Street of the Duchess Anne, until he saw coming toward him with a basket on each arm the fisherman's wife on her way home from market.

Zacharie was afraid she would see him, so he rolled faster and faster till he looked like nothing at all.

"What's that?" cried the old wife. Zacharie whirled past and around another corner and into a gutter of water to catch his breath. But he had not caught more than half of it when he saw a crowd of children. They all shouted together, "Oh, look at the fish for my dinner," and they ran shrieking after him and crying, "I've got him, I've got him!" But Zacharie was too quick for them. He swam and rolled down the hill and along the Street of the Cat Who Fishes and around the corner and

over the cobbles to the Market.

"Oh, what a fish for our dinner!" quacked a duck to a goose and they waddled after him and chased him past the town-crier who beat upon his drum and cried, "A fine fish—"

but Zacharie was
too quick for
them all and
rolled down
the street—

and over the cobbles and around the corner and into the old fisherman clumping home from the port. "Why, that looks like Zacharie," he cried and tried to catch him with his cane. But Zacharie jumped out of reach. "Don't catch me. I'm looking for the sea." He tucked his tail in his mouth and rolled away and left the old fisherman be— hind.

Zacharie rested at the top of a steep hill and looked

out and saw the sea with all the boats on it. He jumped up and down with joy. He took his tail in his mouth and rolled down the hill as

Fast as ever he could and along the quai to the mole and out the mole toward the sea~ ~

and
right
E.L BROCK

under the feet of two red fishermen who were carrying a huge basket of sardines. They stumbled and dropped the basket and the sardines went slipping around every-where and Zacharie was frightened. He made up his mind in one

minute that he would rather be a sardine in a tub than a sardine caught in a blue net out of the big ocean and put in a basket to be cooked and eaten up. Zacharie turned his tail toward the sea and took it in his

mouth and began rolling back the way
he had come as fast as he could - along
the mole to the quai and
up the hill and past
the Market and
down the
Street
of

the Cat
Who Fishes and
around this corner and
that and up the Street of the Duchess
Anne and into the old fisherman's
house and plop! into his own tub.

The old fisherman and his old wife and the yellow cat and the black hen were all sitting around the tub sobbing. But when they heard the plop and saw Zacharie in the water again, they all

began to clap their hands an shou
and mew and cackle. Zacharie splashed back and forth in his tub and bumped his nose against the sides with joy, and they all lived happily ever after.

2627